Miles Gibson was born in a seaside town on the edge of the New Forest. An author of adult fiction and poetry, he is also a screenwriter and artist. When Miles was little, his grandfather used to do clever conjuring tricks – but he never made any Super-Shrinking Powder.

Neal Layton studied Illustration at Saint Martins School of Art. He has won and been shortlisted for the prestigious Nestlé Prize several times and his distinctive artwork features in many award-winning children's fiction and picture books. Neal lives with his girlfriend and a collection of nodding-dog toys.

Little Archie

and the

Tongue-Tingling

Super-Shrinking

Powder

This is Little Archie's first adventure –
but it won't be his last!

Coming soon . . .

**Little Archie
and the
Spectacular
Disaster-Magnet
TV Gadget**

Little Archie

and the
Tongue-Tingling
Super-Shrinking
Powder

Miles Gibson

Illustrated by Neal Layton

MACMILLAN CHILDREN'S BOOKS

First published 2004 as *Little Archie* by Macmillan Children's Books

This edition published 2007 by Macmillan Children's Books
a division of Macmillan Publishers Limited
20 New Wharf Road, London N1 9RR
Basingstoke and Oxford
www.panmacmillan.com

Associated companies throughout the world

ISBN: 978-0-330-44189-6

Text copyright © Miles Gibson 2004
Illustrations copyright © Neal Layton 2004

The right of Miles Gibson and Neal Layton to be identified
as the author and illustrator of this work has been asserted by them
in accordance with the Copyright, Designs and Patents Act 1988.

1 3 5 7 9 8 6 4 2

A CIP catalogue record for this book is available from
the British Library.

Printed and bound in Great Britain by Mackays of Chatham plc, Kent

For Lisa,
who found him
M.G.

For Tiger Wilton
N.L.

Chapter 1

Archie lived with his mother and
father in a small house in the big city.
He had a goldfish and a baby brother.
He called the goldfish Bodger. The
name of his baby brother was Joe.

Archie led a regular life. He had regular meals and regularly cleaned his teeth, owned a regulation pencil box and regularly went to school.

"You have to stay regular," said his mother and father, who made a habit of giving people good advice.

Archie was as regular as clockwork.

He was happy at home but he was even happier when he went to visit his Uncle Bernie.

Uncle Bernie had never lived a
regular life. He lived in a house
called the Jackdaw's Nest. He had
a nose like a raspberry and whiskers
sprouting from his ears.
He lived with his books and
his memories, a parrot
and a gramophone.
He also had a
telescope and
liked to sit
on the roof
at night to
look at the

moon and the stars. He counted the rings of Saturn and looked for signs of life on Mars.

Archie's mother and father disapproved of Uncle Bernie.

"He's a bad influence on the boy," they used to tell each other sadly. "He's barmy and he doesn't keep regular hours."

But Archie liked Uncle Bernie and enjoyed exploring the Jackdaw's Nest.

The rooms were crowded with cupboards and shelves. There were model boats and pictures of bears,

potted plants and crocodile bones.
There were bottles of buttons and
tins of paint and dusty jars of boiled
sweets. There were plans for making
rocket ships and recipes for chocolate
fudge and weather charts of Africa
and maps of mountains on the moon.

Uncle Bernie would often lose one of his shoes in all this confusion and Archie would help him to search the house. The parrot would join them. Sometimes they would find the missing shoe and sometimes they would find something else, like a clockwork

frog or a box of Bengal fireworks. The parrot enjoyed finding sultana biscuits.

After every visit to Uncle Bernie, Archie would go home tired and dusty and covered in cobwebs.

"It's not hygienic," his mother would say, and shake her head and frown.

Chapter 2

The trouble began on Archie's birthday. It was a Saturday. Archie woke up at the regular time and went downstairs to open his presents.

A birthday is an exciting event and

Archie was hoping for surprises:
a conjuring set or a junior detective
kit containing interesting disguises.

But his mother gave him a fountain
pen and a large bottle of ink.

"You can write me a thank-you
letter," she said. His mother liked
giving sensible presents.

Archie's father
gave him a
racing car,
but the batteries
weren't
included.

"You can always pretend," said his father, and went into the garden to look at his cabbages.

His baby brother gave him a smile and did a whoopsie into the potty.

Archie filled his new fountain pen and tried to pretend that the racing car worked, because people expect you to take an interest when you're having a birthday. But he felt a little disappointed.

It was late when Uncle Bernie arrived.

He brought Archie
a present wrapped
in a piece of
blue waxed
paper and
tied with a
length of
hairy string.

"What is it?" said Archie, and
grinned. He picked up the parcel and
gave it a squeeze. He knew it must be
something exciting. He gave it a sniff
and held it against his ear.

"Open it," said Uncle Bernie.

So Archie untied the string and discovered a small glass bottle filled with a yellow powder that glittered when he gave it a shake.

"It's Magic Shrinking Powder," Uncle Bernie said with a laugh. "I found it on my travels in China."

"Is it educational?" asked Archie's mother rather suspiciously.

"Is it suitable for a boy?" frowned his father, holding the bottle against the light.

"What does it taste like?" said Archie.

"It's just for fun," Uncle Bernie

13

warned him. "You're not supposed to

eat it!"

And he laughed again and shook

Archie's hand and then hurried back

to the Jackdaw's Nest to sit on the roof and look at the stars.

Archie put the bottle on the shelf in his bedroom. He crawled into bed and turned out the light. But something strange was happening. He could still see the bottle on the shelf. He blinked and rubbed his eyes. He thought he might have imagined it. He sat up and stared at the bottle. The Magic Shrinking Powder had started to glow in the dark. A soft, golden glow that seemed to fill the room with moonlight.

That's very strange, thought Archie, as he climbed out of bed. He stared at the shining powder for a long time. And then he thought, I wonder what it smells like?

So he took the bottle from the shelf, pulled out the cork and sniffed. It smelt of ginger biscuits, cherry cakes and macaroons.

Delicious, thought Archie. It smells delicious. And then, because it smelt so good, he forgot Uncle Bernie's warning. A taste can't do any harm, he said to himself.

He shook a little of the sparkling
yellow powder into his hand and
gave it a lick. It fizzed and fizzled and
frothed on his tongue.

"Sherbet!" he grinned. And fell
asleep.

Chapter 3

When Archie woke up the next
morning he felt so peculiar that
he knew something must be wrong.
He was buried in blankets and
smothered in sheets, as if the bed had
grown around him.

It took several minutes to fight his way to the surface. He struggled from the bedclothes and climbed on to his pillow. That's not right, he thought. This pillow must have grown in the night. It's huge. It fills the room. It's utterly enormous. But when he looked at himself in the mirror he had the most terrible fright.

He was small.
Very small.

He had shrunk overnight. He was
barely three inches tall.

"What are we going to do with
him?" said his mother when she'd
recovered from the shock. She placed
him in a teacup for safety. "We can't
send him to school – he doesn't fit his
uniform."

"We could sell him to the circus,"
his father suggested hopefully.

"I don't think they do that sort of
thing any more," said his mother.

"Things must have changed since
I was a boy," sighed his father.

"We should take him to Doctor
Morris," said his mother.

So they put Archie in her handbag,
because they were afraid of losing

him, and carried him off to see the doctor.

The doctor peered at Archie and poked him with the end of a pencil. He frowned and scratched his head. He spent a long time looking through the medical books on his desk.

"It's impossible," said the doctor at last. "It can't happen. And if it can't happen, I can't treat him. Take him home and keep him warm. Perhaps he will grow again."

"What happens if he doesn't grow?" demanded Archie's mother.

"You could always sell him to the circus," said the doctor.

They didn't take Archie home. They took him to the Jackdaw's Nest and gave him to Uncle Bernie.

Chapter 4

"Hello," said Uncle Bernie. "What's happened here?" He looked very excited.

He placed Archie on the parrot's perch and peered at him through a magnifying glass.

The parrot grumbled and ruffled his feathers. "I hope he doesn't want my banana," he said.

"This is *your* fault!" said Archie's father, wagging his finger at Uncle Bernie. "You're a bad influence on the boy. Make him grow again."

"And don't send him back until he's normal," said Archie's mother.

Uncle Bernie promised to do his best.

"Don't worry," he told Archie as soon as his mother and father had gone. "I'm sure there's a bottle of Grow-More Powder around here somewhere. All we have to do is find it."

Together they began to search the house for the magic remedy. It wasn't easy for Archie because he was so small and had to be lifted on to the table to search through the jumble of bottles and boxes. He found a dog whistle, a brass button and a box of peppermint balls. The parrot found a trumpet, a toothbrush and a Persian slipper. But they couldn't see anything that looked like a bottle of Grow-More Powder.

Uncle Bernie began to rummage through all the high cupboards and shelves in the room, but the dust was so thick that it tickled their throats and stung their noses.

"Stop it!" shrieked the parrot. "I'm going to sneeze!" He closed his eyes and shook his feathers. He snuffled and shuffled and wheezed

and finally gave a great sneeze that
shot Archie through the open window!

Archie flew into the sunshine with
his arms spread out like wings.

He turned a somersault and kicked
his legs.

He paddled his feet and wriggled his

hands. And, just when he feared he
might hit the ground, he landed in the

brim of a large

lady's hat.

"Help!"

shouted

Archie.

"Help!"

shouted the

large lady.

A man came running and tried to
soothe the large lady's nerves. "What
happened?" he said.

"Something fell from the sky!" said

the large lady, removing her hat and
scowling into the fruit and feathers.

"It's a little bird!" said the man,
pulling Archie

from the hat

and holding

him gently

in his hand.

"My word, but he's an ugly
little chap!"

"I'm not a bird," said Archie
indignantly. "I'm a little boy!"

"Nonsense!" said the large lady.
"Little boys don't fly. We'll take him

to Mr Sprockett. He might have
escaped from his pet shop."

Archie tried to explain what had
happened, but it didn't make any
difference, because when you're only
three inches tall nobody listens to your
opinions. So he found himself wrapped
in the hat and taken to the pet shop on
the corner of the street.

Mr Sprockett rubbed his nose and
peered at Archie and shook his head.

"I've never seen anything like it,"
he said. "It's not a bird. I think it must
be a rare sort of mouse. A very rare

sort of mouse. It probably came from the zoo."

"I'm not a mouse!" said Archie. "I'm a little boy."

"Nonsense!" said the pet-shop owner impatiently. "Little boys don't nest in hats."

He placed Archie in a goldfish bowl with a slice of apple and a string of peanuts, and carried him to the zoo on the other side of the city.

But the head keeper stroked his moustache and closed one eye and said, "It's not a mouse. I think it's a small pink frog."

"I'm not a frog!" said Archie. "I'm a little boy."

"Nonsense!" said the head keeper. He didn't like to be contradicted. "Little boys don't come to the zoo in goldfish bowls. You're an undiscovered frog. You'll be famous. You'll probably appear on television." He dropped Archie into a green glass bottle with a twig and a caterpillar for company. "You'll have to go to the Natural History Museum in America,

where the professors will study you."

"I don't want to be studied," said Archie.

"I'm not going to argue with a frog!" said the head keeper indignantly. "I should be washing the elephants."

He marked the bottle Special Delivery and told the assistant keeper to drive down to the

airport and put Archie on the next

plane to New York.

"Take care of this frog," the

assistant keeper told the captain.

"He's the only small pink frog of his

kind."

Chapter 5

It was a long flight. When the

plane landed in America there was

a limousine with two security guards

waiting to collect the bottle and take

it to the big museum. The traffic was

bad. The weather was hot. When
Archie arrived he was tired and angry.
He sat on his twig and sulked. The
caterpillar had fallen asleep and was
dreaming of being a butterfly.

"I don't think it's a
frog," declared the old
museum professor as soon
as Archie had been
uncorked and placed
in a saucer. "I
believe it's a very
intelligent
mushroom."

"I'm not a mushroom!" said Archie.
"I'm a little boy."

"Nonsense!" said the old professor.
"Little boys aren't found in bottles."

"Mushrooms don't talk," argued
Archie.

"That's why you're so special,"
said the old professor. "We'll have to
send you to the Grand Academy in
Japan. They take a keen interest
in mushrooms."

So the old professor dropped
Archie into a flowerpot filled with
damp straw and told the assistant

41

professor to tell the assistant
professor's assistant to take it to
the airport.

"You've missed the plane to Japan,"
they told the assistant at the airport.
"But Captain Curly's airship is

leaving this afternoon."

So they put Archie into the airship that was moored in a nearby field.

"Take good care of this mushroom," they told the captain. "He must be kept cool and dark."

It took a long time to reach Japan and it was cold flying through the clouds because Archie had to travel in the cargo basket

with the suitcases and parcels. I must
have been around the world, Archie
thought. And I still haven't had my
breakfast.

There was a helicopter waiting
to take him to the Grand Academy.
When Archie was unpacked he was
placed in a glass tank in a room with
Top Secret on the door.

"It's not a mushroom," said the
men at the Grand Academy. They
wore rubber gloves and paper masks.
They were very excited. They peered at
him and scribbled in their notebooks.

"It looks like a very small visitor
from a distant galaxy in space."
They started taking photographs.

"I'm not a distant visitor!" said
Archie. "I'm a little boy."

"Nonsense!" said the president
of the Grand Academy. "Little
boys don't travel in flowerpots filled
with straw."

He paused to comb his hair and have his photograph taken beside the tank. He asked if Archie had a message for the people of Earth.

"Yes," said Archie. "I missed my breakfast."

So they gave him a biscuit and watched him eat it.

"We'll have to send you to someone important who studies the moon and the stars," the president said at last.

"An astronomer," said the vice-president helpfully.

"An astronomer," said the

president. And he placed Archie in a cardboard box marked High Security and sent him down to the harbour with a police escort to put him aboard an ocean liner.

"Take good care of this distant visitor," they told the captain. "He must not be disturbed."

Chapter 6

Archie spent a long time in the box.
It was very dark and uncomfortable.
When the sea was rough he was
knocked and dropped and rolled and
tumbled. And no one talked to him

because the captain had given
instructions that he should not
be disturbed.

Finally the liner docked and
Archie managed to peek through
one of the ventilation

holes in the
box just in
time to find
himself
unloaded
from the ship,

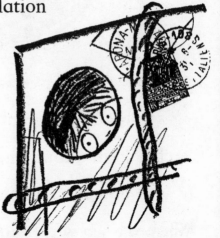

dropped into a satchel and whisked
away by motorbike.

The motorbike sped from the harbour and took the road to the big city.

I'm never going to escape, thought Archie. I shall probably travel in circles forever.

At that moment he felt himself lifted from the satchel, dropped through a letterbox and falling to the floor with a thud.

The box broke open and Archie blinked.

He couldn't believe his eyes. He was back in the Jackdaw's Nest!

"Hello," grinned Uncle Bernie when he found Archie sitting on the floor. "We'd thought we'd lost you."

He was very pleased to see Archie.

He picked him up and took him into the living room.

"Where have you been?" said
the parrot.

"Everywhere!" said Archie.

"I've found the Grow-More Powder.
It was hiding inside my winter slippers,"
said Uncle Bernie, and he held up
a bottle of sparkling green powder.

He mixed a little of the powder with water and helped Archie sip it from a spoon.

"Does it work?" said Archie with a frown. It tasted distinctly of gooseberries.

"I don't know," said Uncle Bernie.

At first nothing happened.

And then Archie felt a strange
tickling sensation in his fingers and
a prickling in his toes. He stretched

and sprouted. He creaked and
gurgled. And slowly, very slowly,
Archie grew back to his proper size.

"It works!" he said, and smiled.

Everyone seemed glad to see
him again. His mother cooked his
favourite supper. His father found
batteries for the racing car. His baby
brother blew bubbles and did a
whoopsie into the potty.

"Regular as clockwork," said his
mother.

"We're back to normal," said
his father.

Peculiar, thought Archie. A most peculiar birthday. And then he yawned and fell asleep.

The End

And coming soon

Little Archie
and the
Spectacular
Disaster-Magnet
TV Gadget

Turn the page for
a tongue-tingling taster . . .

Chapter 1

Archie Bodkin lived with his mother
and father in a small house in the big
city. He had a goldfish and a baby
brother. He called the goldfish Bodger.
The name of his baby brother was Joe.

Archie led a regular life. He had regular baths and regularly combed his hair, owned a regulation lunch box and regularly went to school.

"You have to stay regular," said his mother and father, who made a habit of giving people good advice.

Archie was as regular as clockwork. Every evening, after homework, he liked to sit down to watch TV. He watched Captain Marvellous in Space and programmes containing animals. They were his regular favourites.

Joe – who was only two years old – watched anything he could find by flicking through the channels with the remote control.

He liked all the cartoons, picture puzzles, adventures and comedies.

But magic shows starring Cyril the Clown were his particular favourites. Almost everyone agreed that Baby Joe watched too much TV.

The trouble began one day when Uncle Bernie paid a visit. Uncle Bernie lived in a house called the Jackdaw's Nest. He had a nose like a raspberry and whiskers sprouting from his ears. He lived with a telescope, a parrot and many gadgets of his own invention. He'd invented a talking toaster that shouted at you when the toast was

done, a rocket-propelled skateboard
and a pair of luminous slippers that
were easier to find if you had to get
out of bed in the dark.

Archie loved Uncle Bernie. But his
mother and father disapproved of him.

"He's a bad influence on the boy," they used to tell each other sadly. "His inventions are extremely odd and he doesn't keep regular hours."

Chapter 2

The day the trouble began, Uncle
Bernie arrived at the house with a
special surprise for the family.

"What is it?" asked Archie as they
watched Uncle Bernie struggling

through the front door. He was pulling an enormous parcel made from cardboard and held together with tape and string.

"It's a television," said Uncle Bernie proudly as he unwrapped a strange contraption with lots of dials and buttons and a screen the size of a wardrobe door. The Bodkins looked puzzled.

"We already have a television," explained Mr Bodkin.

Uncle Bernie laughed. "Yes, but this is one of my own invention . . ."

Read the book to find out
just how disastrous
Uncle Bernie's latest invention is!

Perfect for reading while you're
scrubbing the decks, walking the
plank or navigating the open seas.

'It's skull and crossbones
ahead of the other pirate books'
Ship's Parrot

A selected list of titles available from Macmillan Children's Books

The prices shown below are correct at the time of going to press. However, Macmillan Publishers reserves the right to show new retail prices on covers, which may differ from those previously advertised.

Miles Gibson and Neal Layton

Little Archie and the Spectacular Disaster-Magnet TV Gadget	978-0-330-44779-9	£3.99

Martine Murray

| Henrietta (there's no one better) | 978-0-330-43958-9 | £3.99 |
| Henrietta (the great go-getter) | 978-0-230-52884-0 | £6.99 |

Pirate Stories   978-0-330-45148-2   £4.99
Stories chosen by Emma Young

All Pan Macmillan titles can be ordered from our website, www.panmacmillan.com, or from your local bookshop and are also available by post from:

Bookpost, PO Box 29, Douglas, Isle of Man IM99 1BQ

Credit cards accepted. For details:
Telephone: 01624 677237
Fax: 01624 670923
Email: bookshop@enterprise.net
www.bookpost.co.uk

Free postage and packing in the United Kingdom